How Bear Lost his Tail

Retold by Lucy Bowman
Illustrated by Ciaran Duffy

Reading consultant: Alison Kelly
University of Roehampton

Once upon a time, Bear
had a long, thick tail.

The other animals
loved his tail.

3

Bear didn't like it at all.

He tripped over it
when he was walking.

5

Little animals would
even ride on it.

"Bear's tail is better than mine," thought Fox.

8

He decided to play
a trick on him.

9

He crept over to
a fisherman

and took a
few fish.

Fox carried the fish to
an ice hole in the lake.

Bear smelled them.
He came closer.

13

Rumb
Rumble

"Those fish look
delicious," said Bear.

14

"I can show you how to catch them," said Fox.

15

"Put your tail in the hole," Fox told Bear.

"The fish will bite it and you can pull them out."

It may take some time.

Bear waited and waited.

Day became night.

The night grew cold.
It began to snow.

The next day, Fox
came back. Was
Bear still there?

Fox could only see a
huge heap of snow.

"Bear?" he shouted.

Bear jumped up. But his tail had frozen in the lake...

SNAP!

It broke off.

"I'm so sorry!" Fox
cried. "I didn't know
that would happen."

Bear looked at his new
short tail, and smiled.

Bear padded away –
and he didn't trip once.

25

PUZZLES

Puzzle 1

Choose the best speech bubble for each picture.

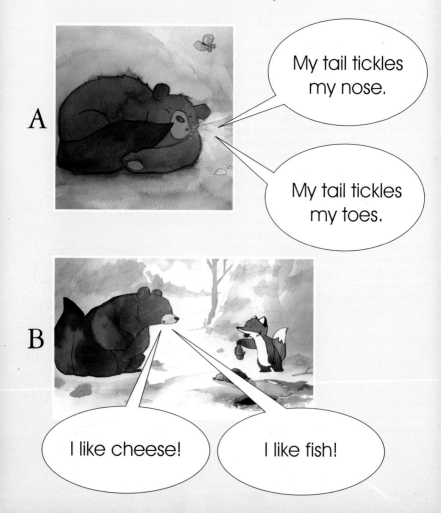

Puzzle 2

Find these things in the picture:

bag	fish	Fox
hat	lake	man

Puzzle 3

Can you spot the differences between these two pictures?

There are six to find.

Answers to puzzles

Puzzle 1

A — My tail tickles my nose.

B — I like fish!

Puzzle 2

hat

man

bag

Fox

fish

lake

Puzzle 3

About the story

How Bear Lost his Tail is based on a Native American folk legend. It has been passed down through the ages by people telling the story to their children.

Designed by Caroline Spatz
Series editor: Lesley Sims
Series designer: Russell Punter

First published in 2012 by Usborne Publishing Ltd., Usborne House,
83-85 Saffron Hill, London EC1N 8RT, England. www.usborne.com
Copyright © 2012 Usborne Publishing Ltd.

USBORNE FIRST READING
Level Three

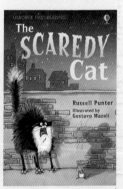

To Jack,
S.McB.

For Deirdre,
A.J.

First published 2007 by Walker Books Ltd
87 Vauxhall Walk, London SE11 5HJ

10 9 8 7 6 5 4 3 2 1

Text © 2007 Sam McBratney
Illustrations © 2007 Anita Jeram

Guess How Much I Love You™ is a registered
trademark of Walker Books Ltd, London

The right of Sam McBratney and Anita Jeram to be
identified as author and illustrator respectively of this
work has been asserted by them in accordance with
the Copyright, Designs and Patents Act 1988

This book has been typeset in Cochin

Printed and bound in China

British Library Cataloguing in
Publication Data: a catalogue record
for this book is available from the
British Library

ISBN 978-1-4063-0453-4

www.walkerbooks.co.uk

GUESS HOW MUCH
I LOVE YOU
—— *in the* ——
SUMMER

Written by
Sam McBratney

Illustrated by
Anita Jeram

WALKER BOOKS
AND SUBSIDIARIES
LONDON · BOSTON · SYDNEY · AUCKLAND

Little Nutbrown Hare
and Big Nutbrown Hare were down
by the river on a summer's day.

On a summer's day there
are colours everywhere.

"Which blue do you like best?"
asked Little Nutbrown Hare.

Big Nutbrown Hare didn't know –
there were so many lovely blues.

"I think ... maybe the sky,"
he said.

Big Nutbrown Hare
looked across the river.
There were grasses and ferns
and tall plants swaying
in the breeze.

"Which green do you
like best?" he asked.

Little Nutbrown Hare began to think,
but he didn't really know.
So many lovely things
were green.

"Maybe the big leaves," he said.

Now it was
Little Nutbrown
Hare's turn to
pick a colour.

He spotted a ladybird, and some poppies.

"What's your favourite
red?" he asked.

Big Nutbrown Hare
thought about red things,
but it was hard to choose
just one.

"I think those
berries," he said.

Big Nutbrown Hare nibbled
a dandelion leaf.

"Which yellow do you
like best?"

There were so many yellows!
Little Nutbrown Hare even
saw some yellows
buzzing about.
How could he
possibly choose?

"Maybe these flowers,"
he said.

Then Little Nutbrown Hare began
to smile and smile.

He looked at Big Nutbrown Hare and said,

"Which brown do you like best?"

And Big Nutbrown Hare smiled too.
There were many many lovely browns,
but one was the best of all...

"Nutbrown!"